It's the Best Day Ever, Dad!

For Chris: Hello, Life!
—Brooke

For my family: the tall, who lift me up,
and the small, who keep me grounded
—Cori

It's the Best Day Ever, Dad!

Text copyright © 2009 by Christa Inc   Illustrations copyright © 2009 by Cori Doerrfeld   Manufactured in the United States of America.   All rights reserved. No part of this book may be used or reproduced in any manner whatsoever without written permission except in the case of brief quotations embodied in critical articles and reviews. For information address HarperCollins Children's Books, a division of HarperCollins Publishers, 10 East 53rd Street, New York, NY 10022. www.harpercollinschildrens.com   Library of Congress Cataloging-in-Publication Data   Shields, Brooke, date.   It's the best day ever, Dad! / by Brooke Shields ; illustrated by Cori Doerrfeld. — 1st ed.   p. cm.   Summary: Sisters Frankie and Violet spend a special day out with their father doing all the things they like best.   ISBN 978-0-06-172445-9 (trade bdg.)   [1. Fathers and daughters—Fiction. 2. Play—Fiction.]   I. Doerrfeld, Cori, ill. II. Title. III. Title: It is the best day ever, Dad! PZ7.S554774It 2009 [E]—dc22 2008032094
Designed by Stephanie Bart-Horvath   09 10 11 12 13 LP/LPR 10 9 8 7 6 5 4 3 2 ❖ First Edition

It's the Best Day Ever, Dad!

By Brooke Shields

Illustrated by Cori Doerrfeld

HarperCollins Publishers

Violet and I wake Daddy up by playing music and doing a dance. We call ourselves the Alarm Clock Girls.

While Daddy shaves, we brush our teeth. Violet needs a stepstool.

Daddy makes pancakes in funny shapes for me and Violet. We like to pretend they can talk. He even makes some special ones for our dog, Darla.

After breakfast we quietly sneak out of the
house. Daddy says Mom needs a day to rest.

Next stop, DOG PARK!!!!
Darla loves the dog park.

Dad teaches me to throw a ball for Darla by putting my opposite foot forward and following through. He yells, "Good throw, Frankie."

When Darla gets tired, we take her home, but we make sure to stop for ice cream on the way.

At home Daddy teaches Violet how to make Darla "sit and wait" before eating her food. I used to feed Darla, but Dad said it was Violet's turn to learn.

When Violet goes down for a nap (she still naps, but I don't have to anymore), Dad and I sit on the couch and watch basketball. I cheer for his favorite team.

I love to sit next to Dad and yell, "Defense!" Sometimes he falls asleep and snores. I take Violet's cozy blanket and I cover him up to rest.

When both Dad and Violet wake from their naps, we go outside and play a game of hopscotch. Dad likes to draw the squares. We even let Darla play.

Playing the game makes us all thirsty (and hungry for a snack), so we love having tea parties in our room. But everybody has to dress up . . . that's the rule . . . even Daddy and Darla! We have named the tea parlor

SISTER CAFÉ.

When the tea party is finished, we like to surprise Mom by cleaning up the room and getting ready for dinner. Dad pretends he is a tickle monster chasing us, so we clean up quickly.

Then . . . the best part of the day . . .

SUPER-DUPER
SPAGHETTI SURPRISE
WITH
THE
FIVE
FAMOUS
CHEFS!

Violet and I make the salad, and Mom and Dad create a new and exciting sauce each time.

We go outside to eat. It's like having
a picnic at our own house!

"Wow. We had the best day ever, Dad!"

Violet and I are exhausted.

Dad kisses us good night and says,

"Tomorrow, we'll go to the beach."